A Week in the Pennines

A Week in the Pennines

B.T. Fisher

Wrate's Publishing

First published in 2022 by Wrate's Publishing

ISBN 978-1-7396165-6-4

Copyright © 2022 by B.T. Fisher

Edited and typeset by Wrate's Editing Services

www.wrateseditingservices.co.uk

A CIP catalogue record for this book is available from the British Library.

To my sister, Sue, for always being there for me.

Part One

Chapter 1
Time for a Change

Tabatha and Arla were good friends at school. After leaving to go their separate ways, they occasionally kept in touch, but Tabatha was surprised when Arla rang with an invite to join her on a week-long hiking holiday in Yorkshire, staying in a self-catering cottage on a sheep farm in the Pennines.

In reality, Arla had booked the cottage in 'Bronte Country' as a romantic surprise for her new boyfriend, Jacob. He was an English teacher at the local grammar school, and he had a particular love of hiking, steam trains and the novels of the Bronte sisters. However, the week Arla booked was in term time and, being a conscientious teacher who was keen to further his career, he refused Arla's suggestion to 'pull a sickie'. Arla would not back down, and as a result the couple parted company. At such a late stage, the cost of the cottage was nonrefundable.

"Oh, Tabby, do come, it will be great to get together

for a catch up. The hiking will be good for you, and there is lots of culture. Haworth was the home of the Bronte sisters. You know, *Wuthering Heights*, and all that. It's right up your street."

This, at least, was true. Like Arla's ex-boyfriend, Tabby was an avid reader of gothic novels.

"And there are several theatres in Leeds, which is also a great place for shopping and museums," Arla continued, reading from her travel brochure. "You work for your dad, so getting time off won't be a problem for you, will it?" she added, accurately anticipating Tabatha's next line of defence. "And I will drive us there. It will help me to get over the split from my boyfriend. I really liked this one."

Tabatha reluctantly agreed. After all, it was only a week, and Arla was fun to be with, albeit a bit manipulative.

Her parents were a bit taken aback when she told them of her intentions.

"Oh, darling, you have never been on holiday without Daddy and me. You won't cope on your own, you know, and why Yorkshire of all places? And in April, too; it will be snowing. I don't think they even have hospitals up there, do they, Daddy?"

Her father said nothing but winked at Tabatha. "I think it's a great idea, Tabby," he whispered to her whilst his wife was in the kitchen making tea. "Arla is a very confident young lady, and you could learn a thing or two from her. I used to enjoy hiking when I was your age. Let's go to the outdoor clothing centre this afternoon and get you kitted out. Mum's the word, though."

As he spoke, Tabatha's father placed his forefinger over his lips and nodded in the direction of the kitchen.

That afternoon, whilst her mother was at the hairdressers, Tabby and her dad went shopping together, where they purchased good stout hiking boots, two pairs of thick socks, an extremely expensive waterproof padded jacket, two pairs of corduroy trousers and a big haversack to carry everything in. When they got home, they smuggled them up to Tabby's bedroom, all the while giggling like naughty children.

Tabatha had always got on well with both her parents, and she tolerated her mother's smothering ways. Tabby's mother was pretty and petite, with blond curls. When she was a child, she had enjoyed going to parties, dancing classes and dressing up. As a teenager, she had had plenty of admirers. Although Tabby had inherited dainty hands and feet from her mum, she had also been landed with her father's lantern jaw. Whilst this was a handsome feature for her dad, Tabatha was constantly aware that it was not such an attractive look for a girl. She hated dressing up, dancing and going to the hairdressers, and she had never had a boyfriend.

Children can be unintentionally cruel to their peers who look a bit different, and Tabatha was bullied when she first started school. It didn't help matters that her mother, who was so vain about looks, was disappointed in her daughter's appearance, and, whilst she undeniably loved her, she was reluctant to take her to parties and other social gatherings where proud mums would be showing off their offspring. Being an intelligent child, Tabby coped well with the situation, but as a result she lacked confidence and did not mix or make friends easily. Her first few days of high school were equally traumatic, until she met Arla. Arla was attractive, outgoing and sociable. She had an older brother and sister and was therefore far more mature and worldly than Tabby, although not as studious and clever. For this reason, Arla needed Tabatha and took her under her wing. The unlikely friends got on well together, with Tabatha helping Arla with her homework and Arla protecting Tabby from the bullies.

Tabby also made friends with Hamish, who was in the same year as her and Arla. Early on, Hamish confided in Tabby that he was gay, but as he did not yet want it to be known, the two of them paired up at school dances and other functions where couples were required. They shared similar interests and the arrangement worked well, meaning school life became bearable for them both. Much later, Hamish became a successful script writer and Tabby occasionally spotted his name in the credits at the end of film or television dramas. This always gave her a buzz.

At the end of their final school term, Arla scraped through her exams well enough to gain a place at university. Tabby had good exam results but chose to stay at home and work in the family business, which she loved. Tabatha's dad owned a sock manufacturing company that had been in their family for several generations. Tabby's grandfather had moved over from the old-fashioned 'socks for gentlemen' to the manufacture of modern synthetic sports socks, and the order books were always full. Tabatha's mum worked part time in the business doing the clerical work and wages, whilst Tabby helped with marketing, sales and dispatches, and filled in anywhere in the factory where she was needed. The current turnover was enough to provide the family with a good living and support their few employees.

∼

Two days before they were due to depart for Yorkshire, Arla rang Tabby at work.

"I've got some really good news for you, Tabs," she said. "Jacob and I have made up and he's taking me to Paris for two weeks in the summer!"

Arla's remaining holiday quota from her job wouldn't stretch to a week in the Pennines as well as a fortnight in Paris, besides which, she didn't want to leave Jacob for a week when they had so recently got back together. "You will be all right on your own in the Pennines," she said. "Have you got a pen handy? I'll give you all the details. You'll have a super time."

Tabatha was stunned. "But Arla, I don't drive, and I

don't know the area at all. I think it's a bit shabby of you to cancel at the last minute. After all, it was your idea."

"I thought you would be pleased for me. Some friend you are! Anyway, it's about time you learned to drive, and to go on holiday without your parents. You are twenty-eight!"

"Oh, just give me the address, then," said Tabatha, trying to sound confident.

"The farmer's name is Mr Boothroyd and the address is Bleakstones Farm, Bleak Lane, Rossington, Yorkshire. Have a lovely time and send me a postcard." With that, Arla hung up.

Tabatha was in tears when she told her dad what had just happened.

"It's not that bad, Tabby," he said. "I think you should still go. You can travel by train, and it will do you good to be on your own for a change. You've got all the clobber now, and it's a very interesting area with lots to do."

"But I don't want to be on my own. Mummy says I can't look after myself! What if I get lost, or robbed, or worse?" Her words tumbled out.

"Your mum doesn't always know best. Why don't you prove to her and Arla that you *can* do things on your own. I promise that if you do get stuck, I will drive straight up to Yorkshire and bring you home."

Tabatha dried her tears and blew her nose hard. She put her arms around her father's neck. "Oh, Dad, what would I do without you?" she said, trying to smile and be positive.

"Come into my office," replied her father. "We will book your rail ticket and I will show you on the map where you are going."

Chapter 2
The Journey

Saturday

Tabatha had been on the train for hours. Travelling from Oxford, the weather got steadily worse the further north they went. Her carriage was full, and she had been in a state of panic all the way. Her haversack would not fit in the rack above her seat, so she'd had to leave it on the luggage shelf at the end of the coach. She was constantly bobbing up and down to check it was still there. Then the guard announced there would be further delays due to the high winds blowing broken branches onto the track ahead. By the time the train stopped at Leeds station it was very late, dark and the rain was torrential. Tabby changed platforms and managed to catch the last departing train to Rossington by the skin of her teeth. She listened carefully to each station announcement, terrified she would miss her stop in the dark. She didn't quite catch the next announcement, but it didn't sound like Rossington, so she relaxed a bit. However, as the train came to a halt, she peered at the station sign through the rain. To her dismay, she realised it *was* her stop. Leaping from her seat, she retrieved her haversack and alighted the train just in time.

The station was unmanned at this late hour, so Tabatha made her way outside and looked around. Her father had told her to take a taxi to Bleakstones Farm. "There are always taxis waiting at train stations, just get in one and tell the driver where you want to go," he'd said.

But there wasn't a vehicle in sight. In fact, the whole place appeared to be deserted. To get out of the rain, Tabatha made her way to a bus shelter. She was trying to quell the rising panic and think rationally when a couple turned into the shelter while laughing and shaking raindrops from their uncovered heads. At first, they didn't notice Tabatha, but when they did, they greeted her warmly.

"Hello, didn't see you there. I think the last bus has gone," the young man said to her.

Tabatha looked the couple up and down. They were both dressed in black, and the man was bald and had tattoos up his neck and the back of his head. There were rings around the edges of both his ears and large, black discs set into his earlobes.

In contrast, the girl had lots of hair, which was piled on top of her head and then draped down her back in thick, matted dreadlocks. She had a ring through her nose and another through one of her eyebrows. "It's a wicked night, and according to the weather forecast, there's more rain to come," she said in a surprisingly cultured voice. She glanced at Tabatha's large haversack. "Are you going far?"

"I'm staying at a holiday cottage, but I'm not sure how far away it is. I was hoping to get a taxi."

The young man promptly took a mobile phone from his pocket and tapped in a number. "Jamil is the local taxi driver," he explained. "His cab office is just a couple of minutes away, but he will come and pick you up here to save you getting a soaking."

He spoke into his phone, then turned to Tabatha. "He'll be here in five!" he said.

Within ten minutes, Tabby was in the back of Jamil's taxi with her bag safely stowed in the boot. She had thanked the couple for their help, and they'd waved her off into the darkness.

"It should take about half an hour to get to Bleakstones Farm," Jamil informed her. "It's up a very bumpy road so I'll have to take it slowly."

After driving on a deserted road up a very steep hill, Jamil took a right turn up a narrow track. "How was your journey here in this weather?" he asked.

"It was OK," said Tabby, "but I nearly missed the station, it was announced as something else."

"Oh, that's because its spelt Rossington but pronounced Roston," Jamil explained.

"Why?"

"Don't ask me, I'm working in my second language!" he laughed.

The track got rougher and steeper, the wind grew stronger and the rain lashed the car so hard that the wipers no longer cleared any water from the windscreen. The taxi rocked from side to side as Jamil slowly picked his way along the track. "There's a farm gate somewhere along here, I seem to remember," he said, "are you OK to leap out and open it?"

Just as he spoke, the headlights illuminated the wooden gate and Tabby jumped out of the cab and rushed over to pull it open. Jamil drove through it and Tabby went to get back in the taxi.

"Oh, sorry, love, you will have to close it as well, to stop the sheep going down the lane and onto the main road."

By the time she had struggled to shut the gate against the wind and hurriedly got back into the car, she was soaked and had several broken fingernails. They continued a short way and arrived in the farmyard. Tabatha could just make out a stone-built farmhouse to the left of the yard. Straight ahead was a large barn with a small cottage attached to it. On the right side, facing the farmhouse, was a row of various outbuildings. The place was in complete darkness.

Jamil pulled up as close to the cottage as he could. "It doesn't look like there is anyone at home," he said, "come on, let's see if the door is open."

He took out a large torch from under the dashboard and they made their way to the little porch at the front of the cottage. Once inside, Jamil tried the door and it creaked open to reveal a small sitting room. Flashing his torch around the walls, he quickly found the light switch and flicked it on. Tabatha immediately spotted a big, old-fashioned stone fireplace laid with paper and sticks ready to light. Next to it on the hearth was a basket filled with logs. The room had a polished, flagstone floor and there was a brown sheepskin rug in the middle of it. Two comfortable-looking sofas faced each other on either side of the fireplace, and over the back of each one was a snowy white sheepskin. Against the wall opposite the fireplace was an oak table, upon which a handwritten note had been placed underneath a box of matches. Tabby picked it up and read it.

Dear Guests,
I was expecting you sooner and I have had to go out. Light the fire if you need to. The water supply is not running so I have left a full water container on the kitchen sink. Be sure to boil it before use.
Also, use the bucket next to the water trough outside for the toilet.
G. Boothroyd

Tabatha turned to Jamil in shock. "You will have to take me back into town," she said. "I can't stay here. I... I can't possibly do that!" She was close to tears.

"What on earth does the note say?" asked Jamil, taking the piece of paper from her hand and reading it out loud. Then he laughed. "What do you think it means?" he asked.

"That I should... you know... wee in a bucket outside," Tabby stammered.

"Come on, I'll show you what he wants you to do!" said Jamil. He picked up his flashlight and led the way outside, back into the teeth of the gale. Just to the right, against the barn wall, was a big stone trough full of clean running water. Beside it was an upturned bucket with a stone on top to keep it from blowing away. Jamil filled the bucket with water from the trough and carried it back into the cottage, through the sitting room and into the kitchen at the back of the house. Tabatha trotted behind him. Jamil set the bucket down and turned on the light. The kitchen was compact but modern with a gleaming cooker, microwave, fridge freezer and washing machine. On the sink stood a full water container, as promised in Farmer Boothroyd's note. A narrow, stone staircase ran up the wall that divided the kitchen from the sitting room.

At the back of the kitchen was another door bearing a sign that said *Bathroom*.

"Here it is," said Jamil. He opened the door, and the light came on automatically. The eighteenth-century house was originally a two up, two down agricultural workers' cottage with very basic amenities. To modernise it for guests, a single-storey bathroom had been built onto the back of the building. Like the kitchen, it was modern but compact, with a handbasin, toilet and an electric shower over the bath. Jamil set the bucket down and lifted the lid of the toilet cistern. Tabby could see that it was empty, and Jamil tipped in the contents of the bucket before replacing the lid.

"There we are," he said, "for the time being, you will have to do that each time you flush."

Tabatha was amazed. "How did you know to do that?" she asked.

"Oh, it happens a lot around here. Most remote properties are not on mains water. Mind you, reading the note properly helped as well!"

"And you're working in your second language, too!" retorted Tabby, and they both laughed.

"Now, are you sure you will be alright here on your own? Besides there being no running water at the moment, there is no TV reception, mobile phone signal or internet connection, and although there is a landline telephone in the farmhouse there isn't an extension here in the cottage. The bus into town passes the bottom of the lane every hour, but the weather forecast is for continuous rain and high winds all week. Mr Boothroyd is a bit grumpy at the best of times, but he will be in the middle of lambing so he will be sleep deprived as well."

Tabatha put on a brave front and insisted that she would be fine. This was mainly because she wouldn't know how to find somewhere else to stay, and she also wanted to prove to her mother, father and Arla that she could fend for herself, if only for one night!

After she paid the taxi fare, Jamil left, and Tabatha watched as his headlights disappeared down the lane into the mist. Panic was beginning to well up in her chest as she lugged her haversack up the stone staircase. She had never slept in a house on her own before, and she was regretting her decision to stay. She peered into the back bedroom, which was tiny and furnished with bunk beds and a small chest of drawers. She began to feel a little better when she opened the main bedroom door and put on the light. The big double bed was made up with crisp, white bedlinen topped with a golden woollen throw. The polished oak floor was partially covered with two sheepskin rugs that had been placed on either side of the bed, and there were thick, gold-coloured curtains at the stone-mullioned windows. The old stone fireplace had been exposed and there was a modern electric fire in the grate. Tabatha switched it on and closed the curtains, making the room feel cosy and safe. She suddenly felt very tired and was surprised to see that it was past midnight. Unable to have a shower, she reluctantly went back downstairs, boiled the kettle, and carried it into the bathroom for a 'lick and a promise', as her mother would call it. She then cleaned her teeth and dashed back upstairs to get into her pyjamas, turn off the fire and climb into bed. Her stomach churned with anxiety, and she wondered how she would get through the next week and whether she should phone her father in the morning.

Chapter 3
Lambing Time

Sunday

Tabby slept fitfully, experiencing anxiety dreams about losing her luggage and getting lost in a swirling mist on the moors. She was awoken abruptly by what she thought was a motorbike starting up outside. It was daylight and she was shocked to see that it had gone eight o'clock. She put on her dressing gown and peered through the curtains into the farmyard below, where she saw a man reversing a vehicle that looked like a large red motorbike but with four wheels. It had a carrier on the front, to which a large plastic bread tray had been tied with bright orange string. Parked in the yard, she also spotted a large, battered, black pickup.

She dressed hurriedly and ran a comb through her short, unruly hair. It seemed to take an age to tie up her boots, grab her warm jacket and open the cottage door.

The wind had dropped but it was still raining and very muddy underfoot.

"Hello, there! Are you Mr Boothroyd?" she called out to the man, while also giving him a wave.

The man did not hear her over the noise of the vehicle, but a big black and white dog did, and it came charging out of the barn aggressively barking. To Tabby's relief, it was on a chain that stopped short in the middle of the yard. The man yelled at the dog, which shot back into the barn, and then he turned towards Tabatha. He was a short, thickset chap with an unshaven, weather-beaten face. She guessed his age to be around the same as her father. He wore waterproof trousers tucked into enormous wellington boots, a much-worn waxed jacket and a tweed cap.

"Hello!" Tabby called again. The man turned off the engine and climbed down from the machine. He came over to the porch, holding out an enormous hand. They shook hands silently and then Tabby invited the farmer into the cottage and out of the rain. He took off his wet coat in the porch, then, to Tabby's horror, proceeded to unfasten the bib of his trousers. He dropped them without even removing his wellies. As Tabby retreated into the living room, he stepped out of them, leaving the trousers still tucked into the boots. Underneath them, and to Tabby's great relief, he was wearing a rather worn pair of jeans and several pairs of odd socks.

"You've chosen an awful week to come here, what

with the weather and the water problem an' all. What's your name, by the way?"

"I'm Tabatha. Why isn't there any running water? There's enough of it about!"

"We're on spring water here and the pump's packed up. I'm waiting for a part. Should be delivered any day. Now, what sort of a name is Tabatha? In these parts, it's a cat's name."

Tabby thought this was a bit rude but decided to pick her battles and pursue the water problem. She couldn't remember ever having to go to bed without first having a bath or a shower. She felt that he was evading the issue.

He looks a bit sheepish, she thought to herself, trying to suppress a giggle at her choice of adjective.

"When exactly did you order the part, and how long will it take to repair?" she asked.

"Well, you know, how long's a piece of string?" he replied without smiling. "I tell you what, if you intend on going into town this morning, I can give you a lift to the bus stop. You can get yourself a nice bit of breakfast. All the shops and cafés are open Sundays with it being a bit of a touristy place, like. I suggest you buy yourself a decent pair of wellies while you're there. They're easier to pull on and off and more waterproof than boots."

He glanced at his watch. "Next bus is in twenty-five minutes!" he announced. Then he stepped back into his waterproof trousers and boots as if they were all one garment. He pulled up the trousers, fastened the bib, put on his jacket and went out into the rain.

Tabby was back in the yard ready to go in ten minutes. She was getting hungry and had made a shopping list, including the wellies and a flashlight.

The farmer was waiting for her in the shelter of the barn door. "Best be quick, Tiddles, that bus occasionally comes on time! My name is Gifford by the way, but people call me Giff."

"What sort of a name is that?" laughed Tabby, and the farmer tried hard to suppress a smile.

He climbed onto the red quad bike, started it up and jerked his thumb towards the pillion seat. Tabby was taken aback; she was expecting to travel in the pickup. Giff whistled to the dog, and they set off down the bumpy lane at speed, with the collie running behind. Tabby was terrified. She closed her eyes tightly and didn't open them again until the machine skidded to a halt.

Peering through the mist and rain, she could just make out the wooden, five-barred gate. By the time she had opened and closed it and arrived at the bus stop with only minutes to spare, her hair and jeans were soaked. The bus arrived and the dog jumped onto the pillion seat that Tabby had just vacated.

"So long, Kitty, I'll meet you off the four o'clock," Giff yelled as she boarded the bus.

~

Rossington was a nice, compact town with lots of interesting shops and cafés.

Breakfast first, Tabby thought, *then welly shopping and the supermarket for provisions.*

On hurrying around the next corner, she almost ran over the young couple who had rescued her at the railway station the previous night.

"Hello again," the girl said cheerily. Today, her hair was bright red, and the long dreadlocks were draped over one shoulder. "We seem to be destined to collide in the rain!"

"I am just going for breakfast," said Tabby, "can you recommend somewhere? No, better still, will you please join me? It would be my treat as a way of saying thank you for last night. Besides, I don't like eating on my own."

In fact, Tabatha had never eaten anywhere on her own before, and she was relieved when the couple readily accepted her invitation.

Once they were all seated in a vegetarian café just across the road, the couple introduced themselves as Hazel and Jeff. Tabby had never tasted vegetarian food before, so she ordered the same breakfast as Jeff. When their food arrived, hers looked just like an ordinary English fried breakfast, with sausage, egg, beans, tomatoes and mushrooms. The only thing missing was some bacon. Jeff explained that the sausage did not contain meat, but he was not sure of the ingredient that made it so tasty.

Jeff was tall and thin. He was dressed all in black, just as he had been the day before, and although he didn't talk or smile very much, Tabby remembered how kind and helpful he had been, and she felt comfortable with him. On the other hand, Hazel was very chatty. She revealed that she was studying English at Bradford University and told Tabby where the best supermarket was and where to buy her wellies.

As promised, Giff met the four o'clock bus on his quad bike, which was now towing a box trailer with the sheep dog sat in it. Tabby reluctantly put her shopping inside the trailer beside the hungry looking collie and climbed onto the pillion seat behind the farmer. He looked tired, and conversation was impossible above the sound of the gale and the noise of the engine. At once, the bike shot off up the steep bumpy lane, almost leaving Tabby behind.

Once back at the cottage, she changed into her cosy new tracksuit and hung her wet clothing over the drying rack in the kitchen. Still feeling cold, she put a match to the fire in the sitting room. After putting her provisions away, she wrapped herself in a blanket and sat miserably on the sofa staring into the fire and wondering how she was going to survive a whole week. For something to do, she unboxed her new torch and fitted the batteries she had bought for it. She switched it on and found it worked a treat. Maybe she would ring her dad tomorrow and he would come and take her home. She was apprehensive about how she would fill the coming days. She enjoyed country walks, visiting museums and going to the theatre, but doing these things on her own, in the rain, held no attraction whatsoever.

Tabby went to bed early and tried to read the local guidebook she had also purchased on her trip into town. It was blowing a blizzard outside, and the strong winds hurled torrential rain against the window. It reminded Tabatha of the storm described by Emily Bronte at the start of her novel *Wuthering Heights*. As she drifted off to sleep with the bedside light on, unwashed and still wearing her tracksuit, she remembered how the story was set in the West Yorkshire Moors.

Monday

Tabatha was awakened abruptly by a massive flash of lightning followed almost immediately by a huge clap of thunder. She glanced at her travel clock; it was four-thirty. She leapt to the window in time to see the sky ignited by forked lightning, which briefly illuminated the hills opposite. The thunder rolled again. A few seconds delay then another lightning strike. This time, the sky appeared to turn green. The crack was louder and her bedside light and all the ones in the yard simultaneously went out. Everywhere was now black.

Still looking down into the yard, Tabby saw a beam of light emerge from the barn. It swung drunkenly from side to side as the person carrying it ran through the rain towards the cottage.

Tabby heard a loud banging on the cottage door.

"Wake up, Tiddles," Giff shouted, "I really need your help out here."

Tabby grabbed her new flashlight and switched it on as she negotiated the narrow stairs. As she wrenched open the cottage door, Giff pushed his way in.

"Whatever has happened? Why have all the lights gone out?" she asked.

"My guess is that the lightning has struck the overhead power cables and there has been a massive power cut," said Giff, "but I needs your help in t' barn. I've got a first time yow wi' twins and the first uns got a leg back. If we don't do summat quick, I'll lose yow as well as the lambs. Put this on with them new wellies and get in t' barn as quick as you can."

Giff threw a pair of worn but clean overalls at Tabby and hurried off, back in the direction of the barn.

Tabby had no idea what he was talking about, but she later learned that a ewe is called a 'yow' in Yorkshire. Giff's first-time yow had not had lambs before and was having difficulties giving birth to twins due to the presentation of the first infant.

By the light of her torch, Tabby pulled on the overalls, which appeared to have been made to fit a giant, rolled up the legs and sleeves, thrust her feet into her new wellington boots, put on her waterproof jacket and ran out into the rain, across the yard towards the barn entrance.

Dawn was just beginning to break, and she could make out the huge open arched doorway. Across the entrance were three wooden hurdles tied together with bright orange string. The inside was lit by a number of bottled gas lamps, which hung from long nails hammered into the walls. She peered inside the barn and waved her flashlight around. About twenty sheep were lying in clean straw in the centre of the space, quietly chewing. Around the sides were about a dozen small pens, each housing a ewe with one or two lambs. A bright light shone from the nearest pen. Tabby saw that Giff was bent over a large pregnant ewe.

"You will have to climb over," he said quietly.

Tabby clumsily negotiated the hurdle and made her way into the pen.

"Climb in, take your jacket off and roll up your sleeves," Giff said briskly, "and hurry up, Tiddles, this is an emergency. These baby lambs need your tiny hands!"

Tabby did as she was told and knelt beside Giff. The sheep was straining now with her head in the air. Her eyes were wide open, and she was grinding her teeth. By the light of his powerful torch, Giff showed Tabby the nose and one pearly hoof of the tiny lamb that was trying to make its way into the world.

"They should be born nose and front feet first, but this uns got its leg back like this," he explained, raising one hand to his nose and placing the other behind his back. "Like this, see? All you 'ave to do is push the lamb gently back and pull its leg forward into the right place. Got it?"

"No, no, I can't do that!" wailed Tabby

"Yes, you can! Put some of this lubricating gel on

26

your hand and close your eyes. Then do exactly as I tell you."

Tabby closed her eyes and Giff guided her hand to touch the nose of the lamb.

"Put your hand in and ease his head back gently. But stop if t' yow pushes. Good, follow his head with your hand until you come to his ear. Now slide your hand down to his shoulder."

Tabby shuddered. It was tight, warm and sloppy in there, and the smell was unpleasant, but she kept her eyes firmly closed and imagined the prettiest, fluffiest white lamb from a children's book.

"Now, try and follow his leg until you get to his knee. Found it?"

"Yes, it's like you said, he's got it behind him."

"Hook your finger behind his knee and try to draw it forward. Got it?"

"Yes, it's a bit tight, though."

Suddenly, as Tabby gently pulled, the little lamb's leg flicked into the correct position and the ewe began to push.

"That's it! I think he's on his way!" said Giff.

Tabby had never felt so relieved.

"Now, move your hand forward and grab both his front legs, pulling gently when t' yow strains. Here he comes, and he is a she! A little gimmer! Er, you can open your eyes now, Tiddles."

The tiny lamb lay on the clean straw. Giff cleared the mucus from its mouth and nose and then grabbed a clean, dry towel and rubbed its little body until it drew a deep breath. Then he gently placed it in front of its mother. She sniffed it carefully and then started to lick it clean.

"She should have another one soon, so you will have to stay around a bit longer just in case. Are you OK? You've gone a bit quiet!"

Tabby spent the rest of the day on the farm. The second twin lamb had been born without much trouble and, much to Giff's delight, it was another 'gimmer'. They were both on their feet and suckling in no time.

For breakfast, Giff made them bacon butties in the farmhouse kitchen, and after they had eaten them, he showed Tabby how to measure and mix milk powder with water to give to some of the baby lambs. There were seven young lambs that needed feeding this way. Giff explained how some of them had lost their mothers; some had been rejected at birth and others were part of a family of triplets. Unlike cows, ewes only have two teats, and so feeding triplets is a bit haphazard. Often, the weakest lamb does not thrive well and is pushed out of the way by its stronger siblings. Tabby learned that these lambs would hopefully be fostered by ewes that had lost their own babies or had only one offspring and were capable of feeding another.

After filling up bottles with the milk mixture, Tabby fed the lambs two at a time. She then helped Giff to fill the feeding troughs with buckets of small pellets called 'ewe nuts', or 'yow nuts' as they are known in Yorkshire. Whilst the ewes were busy getting their fill, the long manger in the centre of the barn had to be stuffed full of fresh, sweet-smelling hay. Tabby was dispatched to fill the water buckets in the individual pens around the edge of the barn, whilst Giff checked the occupants over and fed them hay and sheep pellets. By five o'clock, Tabby was feeling quite hungry herself.

"Give the lambs another bottle, then we can feed and bed t' yows down. Afterwards, you can clean yourself up and I'll get us a curry delivered for supper. My treat for all your hard work. What do you say?"

Tabby admitted that she had never tasted curry.

"You've never eaten a decent Bradford curry? You've never lived!" declared Giff. "The best time to try one is when you're really hungry. I'll order it for seven."

The delivery man from the local Indian restaurant could only get as far as the gate on his little motorbike. Giff told Tabby to drive the quad bike down to meet him whilst he finished off checking the 'yows'.

"But I can't drive that!" she protested. "I can't drive anything, I've never learned."

"How do you know if you've never tried?" asked Giff, jumping on the quad bike.

"Because Mummy told me."

"First lesson tomorrow morning," Giff shouted, as he roared off into the gloom and the rain to collect their supper.

Tuesday

Tabatha enjoyed her first experience of 'a decent Bradford curry' by candlelight. She also enjoyed the cans of lager that followed, but she didn't admit to Giff that although she had tasted beer before, she had never drunk it straight from the can. Giff wasn't very talkative, and when Tabby asked him how many sheep he owned, "a fair few" was the only reply she got.

At midnight, Giff went off to check the ewes and Tabby staggered across the yard through the rain to the cottage. After boiling the kettle for a quick wash, she fell into bed, giggling to herself and feeling a bit tipsy for the first time in her life.

The next morning, however, was a different story. On the upside, the electricity was back on, but her mouth tasted dreadful, and she had quite a headache. Her arms and legs ached from all the lifting and carrying, and her feet were sore from wearing her new wellies. The noise of Giff revving up the quad bike was unbearable, and she pulled the duvet over her head and tried to shut out the world. Recollections of the day before and the suggestion of driving lessons came flooding back, and she suddenly needed the loo.

An hour later, she was washed, dressed and standing in the drizzle in the yard. This time, she had opted to wear two pairs of thick socks.

"Over here, Tiddles!" shouted Giff from the barn. "Even pussycats have the sense to get out of the rain."

Tabby laughed and hobbled over to peer into the

darkness. Giff had erected more pens for the next lot of pregnant ewes, and he was busy filling them with clean straw bedding.

"You look a bit jaded, lass," he said. "Tell you what. If you feed the lambs now, I will give you a driving lesson on the quad before the proper rain starts. At least you will be sat down."

After they had completed their tasks, Tabby climbed on the back of the quad and they drove to an empty field where the driving lessons were to be held. She felt apprehensive as Giff showed her the controls. The vehicle was automatic, and she was put in the driving seat with Giff on the pillion shouting instructions. The vehicle was easier to drive than she had expected, and it was more exciting and very much more powerful. When Giff was satisfied that Tabby would be safe, he left her to practise in the field, after first arranging piles of old tyres and other obstacles for her to negotiate. She spent the rest of the morning roaring around the field, feeling more and more confident. This was the most exhilarating thing she had ever done. When the rain started to come down harder, she negotiated the gate and carefully descended the rough track back to the farm.

In between keeping the fire going in the cottage to dry out her wet clothes, Tabby fed the bottle lambs, refilled the hay racks and water buckets and helped Giff unload bags of sheep feed from the back of the pickup. She soon forgot her hangover.

By six o'clock, the rain was torrential. Giff ordered

them a pizza and Tabby was dispatched on the quad to meet the delivery driver on the main road. She wore a pair of Giff's waterproof over-trousers, and she put the hood up on her padded jacket and fastened it tight. After a few minutes, a taxi approached, stopping when the headlights picked out the waiting vehicle. The driver opened the window to pass through the order and, to her delight, Tabatha recognised him.

"Hello, Jamil," she said. "Remember me?"

"Well, I never! What are you doing on that monster? You will hurt yourself," laughed Jamil. "Just wait 'till I tell Hazel and Jeff what you are up to, they will not believe me. Good on you, girl!"

Wednesday

Wednesday morning dawned. There was no rain today, but it was so misty that Tabby couldn't see across the yard. She had woken early, after a nightmare in which she was running through a field that suddenly turned into a sea of mud. She sank deeper and deeper, the mud overtopping her wellingtons and then swallowing her until she could no longer move. When she finally opened her eyes, she found her bedding twisted firmly around her legs.

The night before, Giff had produced a bottle of red wine, which they shared as they ate their pizzas in front of the wood burning stove in the farmhouse kitchen. This may well have accounted for her nightmares. Having lived on a farm all his life, Giff had a fund of stories and reminisced about local characters and what they got up to. Later, he fell asleep in his armchair, so Tabby boiled the kettle, washed up the few utensils they had used and tidied things away. Giff was still sleeping soundly by the time she'd finished, so she covered him with a blanket and slipped off to the cottage. Still buzzing from the excitement of the day, she made herself a mug of cocoa to drink in bed.

Now she sat up and realised that yet again, she ached all over. A hot bath would have been so welcome. She glanced at her watch; it was six-thirty. She put on the only pair of dry trousers she had left, her last clean t-shirt and a fairly dry fleecy jacket. Then she picked her way carefully down the steep stone staircase and stirred up the fire's embers before adding the last of the dry logs. She soon had it blazing, and arranged yet more damp clothes from the previous day on a wooden clothes horse, which she stood in front of the fire. Next, she took the bucket from the bathroom and ventured out to the trough to fill it. There was no sign of Giff, the dog or the quad bike. *He must have been up early,* she thought.

She had just finished her breakfast when she heard the throaty sound of the quad bike turning into the yard at speed. Looking out of the window, she saw Giff pulling a trailer containing a large crate, upon which the dog was sprawled out. She put on her wellies and rushed across the yard to see what all the commotion was about.

"Look at this, Tiddles, new parts for the water pump!" said Giff.

"How long will it take to fix?" Tabby asked hopefully, briefly fantasising about a long hot soak and a hair wash.

"How long's a piece of string?" retorted the dour Yorkshireman. "You bottle feed t' lambs and chuck some clean straw in for them, then fill t' big feeder in t' barn wi' hay and spread some more clean straw ready for t' next lot o' yows. Meck sure they've all got a drink an all. Then come and find me in t' back pasture and I'll have a special job for thee."

And with that, Giff roared off on the quad with the dog clinging to the crate on the trailer for dear life.

It took Tabby about an hour and a half to fulfil her tasks. Two of the lambs wouldn't take the bottle at first and needed some persuading. She couldn't find a bucket with a handle for the water, so in the end she used the one from the bathroom in the cottage. The barn was empty save for a couple of ewes with tiny lambs in the side pens. Because it had stopped raining, Giff had turned the rest of the ewes and their young out into the lower field. Feeling mighty pleased with herself, Tabby climbed over the hurdles across the barn entrance and hurried off in search of her task master.

"We need t' last lot o' yows from t' moor bringing down and puttin' in t' barn before it starts raining again. We can't put 'em inside whilst they're wet," said Giff, standing chest high in the hole he had dug earlier, revealing the offending water pump. "Teck quad up the lane for about a mile, then you will come to a gate leading to the moor. Fetch 'em all down and get them into t' barn."

"How many are there?" asked Tabby.

"About fifty. If you do that job, I can crack on with t' pump, see?" He turned around and disappeared back into the hole.

"But I can't manage all of them, all that way, all on my own!" wailed Tabby.

"Nay, lass, dog will bring the sheep in; he just can't open t' gate. And take the hurdles in front of t' barn down before you set off." Giff turned away, before muttering from down the hole, "he can't do that himself, either."

"What's his name?"

"Er, Dan, and don't be soft wi' it!"

Tabby returned to the farm with Dan following reluctantly behind. As instructed, she took down the hurdles from the barn's entrance before climbing onto the quad bike.

"Get up!" she told Dan, in a tone she hoped made her sound like Giff. To her surprise, the dog obediently jumped into the trailer. She started the engine and, with mixed feelings of apprehension and excitement, slowly made her way out of the yard and onto the lane leading up to the moor.

The mist had cleared a little and Tabby could now see quite a way in front. The track was uneven and deeply rutted, which meant it was only accessible using this type of vehicle. The gradient was sharp, with high, drystone walls on either side. She felt more confident now and, as she approached the brow of the track, she stood up on the footrests as she had seen Giff do and revved up the engine to negotiate the steep slope that rounded out onto a flat, muddy stretch. The quad splashed through the mud, skidding from side to side with poor Dan bouncing around at the back.

Tabby wasn't sure which field her sheep were in, but she needn't have worried, the dog knew where he was going. He jumped out of the trailer, leapt over the five-barred gate and was off onto the moor before Tabby had turned the engine off. By the time she had dismounted the quad and struggled to open the gate, there was no sign of the dog or any sheep. A few moments later, the first of the ewes began to appear over the horizon.

"Give 'em plenty of space at the gate," she remembered Giff warning her.

Suddenly, sheep poured over the hill like foamy water, with the dog zigzagging behind.

Tabby stood back as they all went through the gate into the lane. "Wait for me!" she yelled in desperation, as she jumped onto the quad and fumbled with the ignition. She didn't want the sheep bolting; there must be no mishaps at this stage. To her surprise, Dan stopped and crouched down. He didn't take his eyes off his sheep, but his ears were turned towards Tabby, awaiting his next instruction. Unsure what to do, she made a clicking noise with her tongue and the dog crept forward, driving the sheep slowly down the track towards the farm.

Tabatha was exultant! This was the most thrilling thing she had ever done. She drove slowly down the track, trying to make the journey last for as long as she could. Giff had warned her that the "yows were in lamb" and told her not to let the dog "run 'em too hard". She needn't have worried; Dan knew his job. By the time she turned into the yard, the mothers-to-be were all safely in the barn pulling at the fresh hay in the manger while Dan sat on guard under the big archway. Tabatha dragged the hurdles back into place across the barn entrance, tied them together with the orange bale twine, called the dog and set off in search of the water pump repair man. She found him still down in his hole in the back pasture. He didn't look up as Tabby and Dan approached.

"How's it going?" Tabby asked.

No reply.

"I can do us both some lunch at the cottage if you like," she suggested, taking the grunt that came from down the hole as a "Yes, please," but feeling a little deflated all the same.

"Oi, Tiddles!" said the hole. Tabby was hoping for some praise at last. "Bottle feed t' lambs first and chuck a bit of straw down for 'em."

An hour later, all the orphan lambs had full tummies and a clean bed. Tabby was back in the cottage opening two tins of game soup that she had bought earlier in the week. She had never had this flavour of soup before, but she'd decided she should at least try some whilst living in the countryside, albeit only on a temporary basis. She had no bread left so she opened a packet of cream crackers, put the pan on the stove to heat the soup and boiled the kettle to make tea.

While at the supermarket, she had also bought half a dozen 'Rossington Fat Ratties', a local version of the 'Fat Rascals' that were sold in the famous Bettys tea shops dotted around Yorkshire. Hazel had assured her that these large, spicy buns, which were a cross between a fruit scone and a rock cake, were typical Yorkshire fare. Originating in Whitby, they were referred to in Shakespeare's Henry IV and were also mentioned by Charles Dickens in his short story *Mother's First Lodger*.

A knock at the cottage door announced Giff's arrival. When he walked in, Tabby was relieved to see he had discarded his muddy wellies and overalls in the porch. There was little conversation and Tabby gathered that the pump repair was not going well. Giff polished off his second helping of soup along with some more cream crackers, which he consumed two at a time. The 'Fat Ratties' went down well too, although Giff said he had never heard of them. Tabby thought they were delicious and made a mental note to take some back home for her mum and dad.

Giff did not linger after lunch. He suggested a list of 'nice sheepy jobs' that Tabby could do for him, explaining this would speed up the repair of the water pump, as it would mean he wouldn't have to keep breaking off from his vital work "restoring hot water for Tiddles!"

Tabatha had worked her way through her list of tasks and was struggling to open a bale of hay to fill the manger when Giff called into the barn. "Come on, Tiddles, come and see this!"

She followed her landlord into the cottage, taking off her muddy wellies and overalls in the porch and leaving the trouser legs in the boots just as Giff had done the first time they met. She'd realised that discarding them in this manner made it much easier, not to mention much less messy, to climb back into them. She hurried through the sitting room and kitchen and peered into the bathroom, where Giff was running the shower. Steam billowed from behind the shower screen, the toilet cistern was filling up and Giff was grinning from ear to ear. "There you are, Tiddles. I will finish your nice sheepy jobs whilst you get yourself cleaned up," he said, "and tonight I will treat you to supper at the Stag Inn." Then, as an afterthought, he added, "providing you sort the lambs out and give 'em their last feed when we get back."

He managed to disappear through the door just as a well-aimed hairbrush came hurtling his way. Tabby could hear him chuckling as he made his way back to the barn.

Taking a shower had never been so enjoyable. Tabby washed her hair and then stood under the gushing hot water for some time. Afterwards, she rummaged through her clothes to find something half decent to wear. Almost everything was either soiled or wet, or both. She brushed the mud off a dry pair of dark green corduroy trousers and matched them with her cream Merino jumper, which she had purposely not worn so far due to the garment's cost. Twenty minutes later, she and Giff were bumping their way down the track in the pickup.

Giff hummed quietly to himself for most of the journey, which Tabby took to mean he was elated about the water pump. Tonight was Singers' Night at the Stag Inn, or the 'Stagger Out', as it was sometimes known. "The landlord usually puts a bit o' supper on," Giff explained.

The pub was busy and quite noisy by the time they arrived. Giff parked up amongst the collection of Land Rovers, pickups and other mud-splattered farm vehicles, and they made their way into the bar. An Irish folk band were performing on a little platform in one corner, and Giff scanned the rest of the room searching for a place to sit. Tabby took in the sea of faces before them. There was quite an assortment; agricultural types with whiskers and tweed caps, some with their black and white collies at their feet; young people seated in groups around the stout wooden tables, laughing and joining in with the singing, and some tourists who had come to hear the music.

Giff spotted a couple he knew. They were sitting together on a bench that ran along the back wall. "Edna, Bob!" he called out. The pair looked up and appeared happy to see him.

Bob, a smiley, stout man with a receding hairline and tweed suit, offered Tabby his seat and he and Giff disappeared to the bar. Tabatha immediately introduced herself to Edna... she did not want to be known as Tiddles to strangers. Edna was a small, round woman with short, wispy grey hair. She was wearing black trousers and a smart, fawn wool blazer over a flowery blouse. The two women chatted amicably. Tabby learned that Bob and Edna were in the middle of lambing, too, but they had two sons to help them.

"Poor Gifford, all on his own," Edna commented. "It's hard work, you know. I didn't expect to see him in here tonight. You're staying in the holiday cottage, aren't you? It's lovely there, and the views are glorious. Are you having a good time? Have you been to Haworth to see the Bronte Museum and Top Withens? Oh, and don't forget the Keighley and Worth Valley Steam Railway. Leeds is so good for shopping, too, don't you think?"

Just then, Giff arrived with a pint of bitter each for Edna and Tabby. "I have ordered you some supper, Tid... er, Tabatha," he corrected himself. "It should be served shortly. I'm just going to take a squint at Bob's new tractor." And with that he disappeared back into the crowd. Tabby eyed the glass full of dark brown beer.

"Not very genteel for ladies," laughed Edna, pointing at it, "but it saves them queuing at the bar." She lifted her glass and took a huge gulp. Tabby asked Edna how many animals Giff had on the farm.

"Bleakstones is all sheep, but a shepherd never says

how much stock he has," Edna informed her, tapping the side of her nose. "We mainly have sheep at Cote Farm, some steer calves and a few bullin' heifers."

Tabby had no idea what a 'bullyneffer' was, and she decided not to ask.

The folk band finished their stint and a girl with a guitar sang some Joan Baez numbers. Tabby tentatively tried the beer. To her surprise, it tasted nice. It was smooth, with a slight, sweet citrus taste. She preferred it to the canned lager she'd had earlier in the week. Then supper arrived. Everyone had the same, and the huge plates were carried on trays and passed around along with cutlery wrapped in paper napkins.

"What is it?" Tabby asked Edna.

"Yorkshire pudding with onion gravy," Edna replied.

Tabatha's mum made Yorkshire puddings most Sundays, but they looked nothing like this. A huge, dish-shaped pudding filled her plate, and inside it was a brown, delicious-smelling stew. Tabby was so hungry she immediately tucked in.

Thursday

Tabby was up early, having slept deeply while dreaming of hot water and clean clothes. After breakfast, she filled the washing machine with as many dirty clothes as she dared to and then stoked the fire ready to dry them.

It was obvious from the bleating coming from the outbuilding where the orphan lambs were kept that they had not had their morning feed, so she set to mixing the milk powder and filling the bottles. As she crossed the yard, she noticed Dan sitting alertly by the hurdles in front of the barn, which indicated that his master was inside. After feeding the lambs, she walked over to the barn entrance and casually looked inside. Several babies had been born to the ewes that Tabby had brought down from the moor. Giff was holding one of them, and in his free hand was clutching a weird implement.

"What are you doing?" Tabby enquired.

"Trust me, Tiddles, you don't want to know!"

After assuring Giff that she was keen to embrace all the lambing tasks, Giff gave Tabby a master class in tailing and castrating newborn lambs. He explained that tail-docking was necessary to help avoid flystrike during the hot weather. This condition is caused when flies lay their eggs on another animal, and Giff had witnessed firsthand the devastation that maggots can cause to a sheep's fleece. In addition, all the male lambs, or 'tup lambs', as Giff called them, had to be castrated to prevent them from mating the ewes; this job was reserved for his pedigree rams. Both the docking and castrating functions had to be carried out as soon as possible after the lambs were born. Giff said how his father had told him that traditionally, shepherds would bite off the lambs' tails. Tabby wondered whether they did the same to the other appendage as well, but she decided not to ask.

The rest of the day flew by. Giff drove the quad

bike out to the top pasture, with Tabatha on the pillion and Dan in the trailer. A fence had recently blown down in the gale, so they took with them tools, fence posts 'and a roll of wire netting. With Dan staying well out of the way, Tabby held the fence posts, keeping her eyes firmly closed whilst Giff drove them into the ground with a huge mallet. After securing the netting to the posts, Giff let Tabby drive back to the farm and commented how impressed he was with her progress. By the time she returned to the cottage, she had forgotten all about her washing, which was still in the machine, and the fire she had stoked up that morning had gone out.

Friday

When Tabby awoke on Friday morning, the sunlight was streaming in through the partly open curtains. She went to the window and gazed out. Instead of the usual grey view of mist and driving rain, she could see right across the valley. This must be the lovely view that Edna had spoken about. Several old, stone-built farms, just like Bleakstones, stood on the opposite hillside. The surrounding green fields were divided by grey stone walls, and they were dotted with grazing sheep and lambs enjoying the sunshine. Birds soared over the moors beyond, in a sky made up of delicate shades of pink, turquoise and purple. It was indeed stunning.

Tabby hung her wet clothes out to dry on a washing line she had discovered behind the cottage. She hoped they would dry quickly; after all, she had to pack everything ready for her journey home.

She had just finished pegging out when Giff knocked on the cottage door. "Come on, Tiddles, put your wellies on, we're off for a ride!" he shouted. Although slightly taken aback by the apparent change in the dour Yorkshireman, Tabby readily obeyed and walked out into the sunshine and a completely different world. The sky above was blue, and there wasn't a rain cloud in sight. The soft breeze brought the lovely clean smell of grass and spring flowers. Birds were singing and the lambs were bleating. It was so crisp and clear that you could see for miles.

"I'm taking you on a picnic," said Giff, holding up a carrier bag bearing the logo of the local agricultural supplies store. "Jump on board." He jerked his thumb towards the waiting quad bike. Tabatha took note of the trailer behind it, which had been filled with bales of hay and a full bag of 'yow nuts', as Tabby now called them in the true Yorkshire tradition. As always, the dog was on top of the cargo. Tabby realised this was not just a pleasure trip.

Sure enough, Giff took the loaded trailer into the pasture with the ewes and lambs, and together they filled the hay manger and tipped some of the sheep pellets into the feeding trough whilst Dan stood guard at the gate. The mums pushed their way up to the trough to eat their share, their lambs gambolling and skipping along behind. After a quick head count, off they set again. The dog jumped into the trailer and

Tabby closed and secured the heavy wooden gate before climbing onto the seat behind Giff. They continued the routine in the next field, which held the 'tups'. These were young rams that would be going off to market. "Got to get 'em a bit bigger first," Giff explained.

He noticed one of his tups was limping badly on his front leg. "He needs lookin' at, we can pick him up on our way back," he said, and off they went again.

This time, they went right up onto the moor. Although the sun was shining, the ground was still wet and Giff seemed to enjoy skidding and splashing through the puddles, which made Tabby squeal with delight. Eventually, they came to a halt at the very highest point of the moor. Giff pointed out Pen-y-ghent in the distance and explained that this prominent and distinctively shaped peak was the third highest fell in the Yorkshire Pennine range.

They climbed off the quad, and Giff led the way to the shelter of a group of huge Millstone Grit boulders. Tabby sat with her back against the warm stone and closed her eyes. It felt so tranquil after the dreadful weather of late, and all her anxieties floated away. She was even looking forward to the challenge of the journey home, which up to yesterday she'd been dreading. When she opened her eyes again, she saw that Dan had curled up against her outstretched legs, which she took as a great compliment.

From his carrier bag, Giff produced a badly wrapped parcel, which he unfolded and proffered to Tabby. On closer inspection, the contents appeared to resemble sandwiches. They were what Tabby's mum would describe as 'doorsteps'.

"A good Yorkshire workhouse butty," said Giff, as if reading her thoughts. "Corned beef and piccalilli."

Tabby tucked right in; she was hungry, and the sandwiches were delicious, if a bit heavy on the piccalilli. Chewing slowly, she surveyed the beautiful view before her. Was it worth waiting all week for this? Yes, definitely. Tabby decided she wouldn't have missed it for anything.

She still had half a doorstep left to eat when Giff and the dog both jumped up. "Come on, Tiddles, look sharp," said Giff, "we'll have to pick up that tup on the way home. When we get back, I'll take a gander at his foot while you hay up the yows and bottle feed t' lambs. Then we'll bed them down a bit early; we are having guests for tea!"

Tabby crammed the rest of the sandwich into her mouth and jumped onto the quad, her mouth too full to argue. She had just finished chewing when they reached the tup field. She opened and closed the gate and helped Giff to drop the ramp down on the trailer. They put a hurdle at either side of it, creating a route that the lame sheep wouldn't be able to escape from. Giff instructed Dan to separate the animal from the rest of the flock and drive it towards the trailer. The sheep looked suspiciously at the opening and reluctantly limped up to the ramp. All was going well until, to everyone's surprise, including the dog's, it suddenly turned towards Tabby and charged.

"Grab it!" ordered Giff.

Tabby threw herself at the sheep. She was intending to hold it around the neck, as she had seen Giff do, but although it was a young animal, it was fully grown and powerful, and her arms slid down its shoulders and she almost fell onto its back. Her hands slipped over its rump and down its back leg. She managed to clutch her hands around its hock, just above the hoof, but she was now lying full length on the ground and her prisoner, desperate to join its friends, started dragging her along in the mud.

"Don't let go!" yelled Giff, running over to help. He grabbed the sheep around its neck, and between the two of them and Dan, they managed to manoeuvre the animal into the trailer. Tabatha was covered in mud from her head down to her wellies, and she looked worse than if she had been dragged through a hedge backwards.

"Should have put overalls on!" was all Giff said, as he started up the quad bike's engine.

"I was told that I was being taken on a scenic tour and a picnic, not for a mud wrestle with a ram!" retorted Tabatha, while surveying the state of her expensive padded jacket. "I've got to wear this to go home in tomorrow!" she complained.

"Don't worry, lass. The mud will come off when it's dry," Giff reassured her.

It transpired that Giff had invited Edna and Bob for dinner. To Tabby's surprise, he was a good cook. His mutton in red wine was delicious and served with piles of perfectly cooked fresh vegetables. For afters, Edna brought a homemade apple pie, which they had with thick cream. A selection of cheeses followed, accompanied by a decent bottle of red brought by Bob.

"What do your parents do?" asked Edna after it had been established that Tabby still lived with them.

"They knit socks," Tabby replied. The dinner table fell silent, and Bob, Edna and Giff exchanged glances. "We have a small business manufacturing sports socks," Tabby hurriedly explained.

"Pure British wool I hope," said Bob, and both Giff and Edna nodded.

"I'm not too sure," stammered Tabby, who knew full well that all their socks were synthetic. But she didn't want to get into a heated discussion. Giff got up to fetch more wine from the kitchen.

"Have you got a boyfriend?" asked Edna, changing the subject. "Our Alun has a nice girl; I forget her name. Our Robert hasn't, though. Nice lad. You'd like him, wouldn't she, Bob?"

Just then, Giff appeared in the doorway behind Edna and Bob. Upon hearing this remark, he feigned an expression of horror, shook his head vigorously at Tabby and made a cutting motion across his throat with his hand. Tabby had to look away for fear of giggling.

"He's a big lad, there's no doubt about that," Bob commented with a sigh.

At this, Giff nodded franticly, blowing out his cheeks and raising his shoulders and hands in an expressive gesture.

Tabby bit her lip and turned to focus on Edna. "Have you ever made Fat Ratties?" she asked her.

The rest of the evening passed uneventfully. The conversation was mostly concentrated around auction prices, the cost of animal feed and extortionate veterinary bills.

"That new brand of lamb milk powder that your Alun recommended is cheaper, and it don't go lumpy like t'other stuff," commented Giff. "The lambs take it well an' all, don't they, Tab?"

Tabby nodded in agreement, happy to have been asked her opinion, even though she had no experience of 't'other stuff'. She felt included, relaxed and happy. Suddenly, she didn't want to think about going home.

Bob and Giff continued to talk farming whilst Edna wrote out her recipes for giant Yorkshire puddings and Fat Ratties from memory, which she gave to Tabby to take home with her.

After Edna and Bob had said their goodbyes, Tabby helped Giff to clear away and wash the pots.

"You have been such a big help to me this week, Tiddles, as well as putting up with no water and the power cut. To say thank you, I would like to give you a week's free stay in the cottage. Luckily, I have a vacancy at the end of June. What do you say?" Giff asked casually.

Tabby didn't need long to decide. Imagining sunny

skies, hot water and seeing all the sights she had missed, she agreed and thanked Giff for the offer.

"That's settled, then," he said, before adding, "I've got the shearers coming that week. You'll enjoy shearing, Tiddles!"

Giff and Tabby spent the rest of the evening and into the early hours in the lambing shed. Giff dealt with a prolapsed ewe, whilst Tabby lambed twins all on her own. Just as she'd managed to get them both to suckle, a further emergency arose, and so it went on until dawn broke. Another ewe with newborn twins developed mastitis, so her lambs were introduced to a foster mother, whose own lamb had sadly died. She had lots of milk but obstinately refused to feed the interlopers. Tabby helped Giff to tube feed the weak lambs with warm colostrum, which he had taken from another ewe. Tabby held each of the tiny lambs in turn whilst Giff gently passed a rubber catheter through their mouth, down their throat and into their stomach. He then carefully poured a small amount of the liquid into the funnel attached to the tube. Tabby could feel each of the lamb's tummies warming up. Giff explained that the colostrum, which is the first form of milk produced by a mammal, contained antibodies that would give the lambs some immunity to disease and the best start in life. Afterwards, he fastened the foster ewe into a gate-like contraption, which trapped her by the head. In theory, this would enable the lambs to suckle. Tabby was left in the pen, guarding the lambs from being kicked by the irate foster mother and trying to encourage them to suckle.

"Keep at it," Giff said. "She will take to them once her own milk has gone through them."

Part Two

Chapter 4
The Journey Home

Tabby managed to grab an hour's sleep before her alarm went off, awakening her from a deep, exhausted slumber. She'd dreamt that she was trying to catch the tup in the field, but when she finally managed to grab it by its back leg, the leg came off in her hand and it ran away on the other three.

An early start was needed to catch her train to Leeds, and she looked forward to sleeping all the way home. She was so glad she had already done her packing.

She had just finished her breakfast when Giff called from the yard, "I have got summit for thee, Tiddles!"

She sleepily staggered outside, where Giff presented her with a rather battered shepherd's crook made from aluminium. It was almost as tall as she was, and at some point in the past, it had clearly been run over by the tractor.

"Now you are a real shepherd!" said Giff. "When

you're ready, I'll take you to the station. I have to call at the agricultural suppliers nearby anyhow."

Tabby felt quite sad about leaving the farm, especially as she said goodbye to the twin lambs and their foster mother and wished good luck to the remaining mums to be. She fed the tup with the bad leg an armful of sweet hay and bid farewell to Dan, the dog she had been so frightened of when she first arrived. He gently licked her hand.

By the time Tabby had done all this and opened and closed the gate in the lane, she was a little grubby. She had hay in her hair, her feet were muddy and her fingernails were black, but she didn't care.

Giff drove them towards the town in silence. He was as tired as Tabby, but he still had a long day ahead of him. He kindly waited outside the bakery whilst she purchased half a dozen Rossington Fat Ratties to take home for her parents. When they arrived at the station, it appeared to be quite busy. Tabby was still early for the train, which was a good thing because carrying a box of Ratties, her haversack and the battered crook was no easy feat.

"See you in June, Tiddles!" Giff shouted out of the window, before roaring away in a cloud of exhaust fumes and leaving a trail of straw in his wake.

Tabby felt a little self-conscious as people turned to stare at the person who had arrived amid such a commotion. Then, slowly but surely, she began to recognise some faces. Hazel and Jeff were standing at the bus stop and waving to her. Hazel was wearing a lime-green kaftan that matched her lime-green hair, huge gold hoop earrings and dark sunglasses. Standing with the couple was Edna and her son Robert, Edna having taken advantage of the chance to introduce her son to Tabby. At six foot tall, he was a giant of a lad, and his tweed cap only just fit on his large head. His podgy cheeks were fiery red, and he appeared to have no neck; his face and enormous body seemed to be all one. He gave Tabby a shy smile as she walked over to them. "Hello everyone, are you going into Leeds?" she enquired.

"We have come to see you off," said Edna. "This is our Robert," she added, pushing the bashful lad towards Tabby with such force that he almost bumped into her. He became flustered, and his face glowed even redder.

"I like your hat!" said Tabby, not knowing what else to say.

Just then a taxi roared into the station yard, parked up rather haphazardly, and Jamil jumped out. "Hello, you lot, I thought I had missed the departure!" he said. "I can't believe you survived the week, Tabatha, I was expecting a call any day saying, 'Please, please take me home, I won't stay here another day!'" Jamil mimicked Tabby's home counties accent.

Tabby was so pleased to see him. After all, he had made the whole week possible. "I will be back in June," she said. "Giff has offered me a vacant week at the cottage."

Her goodbye party exchanged amused glances.

"Whaaat?" asked Tabby.

Robert spoke for the first time. He had a surprisingly high falsetto voice. "Isn't that the week he keeps free because of the shear—" a dig in the ribs from his mother prevented him from finishing the sentence.

"Just watch out Giff doesn't offer you a week at Tupping Time," said Jeff, and the lads all chortled. Edna looked at them sternly, but Tabby smiled in ignorance.

"Train!" yelled Jamil, grabbing Tabby's haversack.

Edna gave her son another great shove. "Help Tabatha with her box and give her your letter!" she said.

Robert took the Fat Ratties from Tabby, and they hurried after Jamil onto the platform. Tabby turned and waved her crook to her laughing group of new friends and ran after her luggage carriers.

Jamil heaved her haversack into the luggage rack and Tabby climbed aboard. Robert, who was out of breath from the sudden exertion, handed over the box of Ratties and an envelope. "Mum said to give you this," he mumbled as the stationmaster blew his whistle. The train door closed, and Tabby stuffed the letter into her pocket.

"Thank you for everything," she called to Jamil as the train pulled away. Tears rolled down her cheeks.

"See you in June," he mouthed to her, and she watched through the window until he, Robert and the station had disappeared from view.

The train was almost empty, and Tabby sat near the luggage rack so she could keep an eye on her haversack and shepherd's crook. She'd imagined she would be tired, but she was buzzing with excitement. She thought about Jamil and how witty, capable, practical and dependable he was, and about his lovely, deep brown eyes and ready smile. He had been her knight in shining armour. She was really looking forward to seeing him again. For now, she couldn't wait to tell her parents all about her adventures, though as she relaxed into her rather worn seat, she began to feel a bit teary again. She reached into her pocket for a tissue and her fingers touched the letter Robert had given her. She opened it with some trepidation.

Dear Tabatha,
It was nice to meet you today. We have no internet
connection at our farm so I would like to be your pen
friend. If you want to write to me, my address is:
Cote Farm, Long Lane, Rossington, Yorkshire.
Hope you have a safe journey home.
Looking forward to hearing from you.
Yours sincerely,
Robert Batley

Tabatha folded the letter and put it back in the envelope with a sigh. She didn't wish to hurt Robert's feelings and vowed to think carefully about how to respond when she got home. She sent a text to her father to let him know where she was.

Leeds station was a great contrast to Rossington. It was enormous and bustling with people who all seemed to be smartly dressed and in a hurry. Tabby headed for the escalator to change platforms. She only had a few minutes before her train was due to depart. Her appearance attracted lots of stares, but she was now too tired to care. She hoped for a nice quiet carriage where she could sleep all the way home. Her parents were meeting her at the station, and she was aching to see them.

When the train stopped at the platform, it was just as packed as it had been on the journey up. Tabby had reserved a window seat and set about trying to find it, only to discover it was occupied by a middle-aged man with a paunch. He was leaning against the window and appeared to be asleep, but on closer inspection Tabby could see that he was peering at her behind his almost-closed eyelids. She checked her ticket again against the number on the back of the seat.

"Excuse me, this is my seat, I'm afraid you will have to move," she said politely. There was no response apart from the eyes closing tightly. The aisle seat was occupied by a smart looking woman around Tabatha's age. She smiled sympathetically at Tabby and then nudged the man in the ribs. "Oi, mate, I know it's a bummer, but you will have to shift yourself!" she said in a pleasant, sing-song voice.

"Who says?" said the man, without moving.

"I do," replied the woman, and with that she stood up. She must have been over six-feet tall, and although not overweight, she was certainly packing some muscle. "I'll help you if you like" she said, taking the man's arm in a mock kindly manner. "Up we get!"

With that, the man was yanked from his seat and firmly put in the aisle. He stuck out his lip as if he was going to protest, then thought better of it, retrieved his laptop and hurried off up the corridor.

"Thank you so much," said Tabby, putting her crook and box of Fat Ratties in the overhead luggage rack and squeezing into her seat.

"You are welcome," said the lady, taking the seat beside her. "I travel this route regularly and I'm always coming across his type. They don't bother to book a seat, and either pretend to be asleep or are just downright rude and aggressive. Are you a shepherdess?"

"Well, I was for a week, but I am going back home now," replied Tabby. "What do you do?"

"I'm a hydrography and meteorology specialist officer in the Royal Navy," the woman replied. "I have been on home leave for a couple of weeks and stayed with my mum, but now I'm going back to join my ship."

"Wow!" was all Tabby could say.

Being so sleep deprived, Tabby dozed off almost as soon as the train left the station. When she awoke two hours later, the carriage was almost empty, and the naval officer had gone. Tabby felt refreshed and wide awake.

She combed her hair and tried to make herself look more respectable to meet her mum and dad.

Tabatha's parents arrived at the station early, and they had been standing on the platform for a good twenty minutes by the time her train arrived. Tabby's mother, who was behind their early arrival, was now in a state of high anxiety. She hurried along the carriages towards the front of the train, frantically peering through the windows and doors while saying, "She's not here, she must have got lost. Where is she? Did she even make the connection? I knew this would happen; I said it would! She should never have gone away on her own."

Tabby's dad saw his daughter alight from the back of the train carrying her huge haversack. Meanwhile, her mother was running in the opposite direction. He waved, strolled over to her and kissed his daughter on the cheek. "Hello, you! Had a good time?"

"Oh, yes, it was super. I have loads to tell you! Where's Mummy?"

"She thinks you have missed the train, and she's gone to give the driver a good telling off for leaving you in Leeds!" her father laughed, as he took the haversack. "What's that you've got there?" he asked, pointing to her battered shepherd's crook.

Before she could answer, her mother came tottering over all out of breath and red in the face. She threw her arms theatrically around Tabby and cried, "Oh my baby, my baby, safely home at last!"

Tabby and her father edged her gently out of the station and into the car. With Tabby's belongings safely stowed in the boot, they drove home, her mother alternately chatting and crying.

Back at the house, over a cup of tea and some rather crumbled Fat Ratties, Tabby broke the news that she would be returning to Yorkshire in June. Her mother dramatically ran wailing from the room.

"She will be fine, you go and enjoy yourself," said her dad. "You have come back a different person."

"Oh, I know," said Tabby. "But just one thing, though, Dad. What happens at Tupping Time?"

Over the next few days, Tabby was extremely busy. Much to her mother's further dismay, the first thing she did was to book a course of driving lessons. She then wrote a short note to Robert to tell him she had arrived home safely. Arla phoned and asked Tabby how she had managed on her own.

"Oh, you know, I had a lovely time. The weather was awful, but—"

"I'm so glad," Arla interrupted, "we must have a proper catch up soon, and I need to borrow your copy of *Wuthering Heights* to take to Paris with me. I want to make the right impression on Jacob!"

They arranged a date to meet up, and Tabby shook

her head and smiled as she put down the phone. *She never changes!* she thought with affection.

Tabby also spent a lot of time on her laptop researching the availability of woollen sock yarn. Back in the factory, she called a meeting with her father, their machine engineer and the marketing manager to discuss the possibility of converting a machine to produce hiking socks made from British wool. She got in touch with several Yorkshire spinning companies to check the supply and price of suitable yarns. With the costings and availability favourable, it was decided they would give the hiking socks a go. Tabby decided on natural colours, and they would market them as the 'Bleakstones Range'.

A week or so later, Tabby received a letter from Robert. It was mainly about how well the lambing had gone, what was happening on the farm and how his dad's new tractor was making life so much easier.

The letter ended: P.S. Jamil has a wife.

Tabby bit her lip, surprised at how perceptive Robert was. *Well, that's that, then,* she thought with a disappointed sigh.

Chapter 5
Shearing Time

Tabatha did return to Bleakstones Farm in June, primarily to help with the sheep shearing. The weather was just right for the task; dry but not too hot. The three-man sheering team were from New Zealand, and they were travelling around the UK shearing flocks, mainly for hill farmers like Giff and Bob. Tabby helped Giff to clean the barn and get it set up for their arrival. To make things easier for them, they used hurdles to create holding pens, with a one-way system for the sheep, which were gathered in the big field next to the farm.

Giff explained that most sheep are shorn annually. "Stops 'em getting dagged up," he said.

Tabby was none the wiser. Robert explained to her later that if a sheep's fleece becomes soiled with faeces, it could result in flystrike and maggots, which posed a big danger to the animal if it wasn't dealt with quickly enough.

On the morning of the shearing, Tabby was woken at five o'clock by the sound of bleating outside. She was up and dressed in no time. She now had her own overalls, and at Robert's suggestion had invested in some steel toe-capped boots.

The shearers arrived at seven in a hired camper van, where they slept and travelled from farm to farm. Bob, Robert and Alun followed them up the lane in their Land Rover. Tabby was surprised to see that Robert was much fitter and had lost some weight. He wasn't wearing his cap and his dark, curly hair was well cut. He looked much happier and more confident than when she had last seen him at Rossington Station back in April.

Within ten minutes, the shearers had set up their electric clippers, put on their special footwear and were giving a haircut to the first three sheep.

Robert showed Tabby how to present the fleece to make the most of the clip. He spread it out on a clean board, laying it flat with the cut side down and the tail end nearest to him. First, he removed and discarded the soiled parts from around the sides, then he folded in the edges and rolled it up tightly. Finally, he made a small hole, into which he neatly tucked the piece shorn from the animal's neck, which secured the bundle.

"Wrapping the fleece this way displays the shoulder wool," Robert explained, "which is the best wool on the fleece. The grader at the British Wool Marketing Board will examine it, and hopefully we will get the best price for our clip."

He left Tabby to continue wrapping with Bob, while he went off with his brother Alun to help Giff to gather the sheep to ensure a constant flow for the shearers.

Bob and Tabby had a wooden board each, and it was backbreaking work. They had to work quickly to keep up with the three shearers. As soon as one fleece was wrapped, another one had been tossed onto the board to be cleaned up and rolled. The board had to be regularly swept clean and the wool bundles packed tightly into enormous bags that were due to be collected later by the British Wool Marketing Board.

By midday, all the sheep had been sheared, and they were back in the meadow looking as white as freshly laundered sheets. They were also bewildered, vocal and looked much thinner than before.

Edna and Alun's girlfriend, whose name still remained a mystery, had prepared a big lunch at Cote Farm. The spread included huge plates piled high with sandwiches, home-cured ham, Wensleydale cheese, egg and cress, and a huge assortment of homemade pickles and relishes. Tabby went into the kitchen to offer her help.

"No, no, Tabatha, you sit there next to our Robert," said Edna, pulling the empty chair next to her son out from under the table. Tabby sat down with an embarrassed glance towards Robert as Edna bustled off.

"Sorry about me mam, she is determined to marry me off!" said Robert. "Actually, Tabby, I have met someone special. Her name is Andrea, but I haven't told me mam yet as I don't want her frightening Andie off!"

"Oh, I am so pleased, Robert," said Tabby, suddenly realising the reason behind Robert's new look. "I do hope it works out for you both, and by the way, thanks for tipping me off about Jamil before I made a complete fool of myself, you are a good friend."

They grinned at each other and Tabby thought what a lucky girl Andrea was.

After lunch, the same shearing system was deployed at Cote Farm. Alun's girlfriend came to help Tabby with the wrapping but quickly lost interest and kept nipping off for a smoke or a drink. Tabby was getting tired, and the fleeces started to back up. Luckily, Giff came to her rescue, and between them they soon caught up. By seven o'clock that evening, all the bulging fleece bags were sewn up ready for collection, and everything had been put away.

As the shearers were moving on in the morning, Edna had roasted a huge leg of home-produced lamb in her Aga, which was carved and served with all the trimmings, including roast potatoes, carrots, peas, mint sauce and, of course, Yorkshire puddings and gravy. A huge rhubarb crumble with an enormous jug of custard was brought out for dessert. Afterwards, the shearers carried in two crates of lager to share. Bob played the piano and Tabby and the shearers were taught the words to the song *On Ilkla Moor Baht 'at*. In return, the three New Zealanders tried to teach everyone their version of the Haka. Then Robert, who had a lovely singing voice, gave a rendition of the hymn *The Lord My Pasture Shall Prepare. And Feed Me With A Shepherd's Care*, which almost brought everyone, including the shearers, to tears. It was a memorable evening.

When Tabby returned home on the following Saturday, her father was pleased to see her, but her mother seemed offhand and upset. "I hope you haven't planned any further visits to Yorkshire," she said. "I am fed up with all the extra washing every time you come home. All your clothes are so soiled and smelly. And we have been incredibly busy at the factory after being inundated with orders for woollen hiking socks... and that's your fault as well!" she complained.

Chapter 6
Party Time

Since returning from the Pennines, Tabby's confidence had grown by the day. She passed her driving test the first time and bought herself a little car.

Over the next year, she worked closely with her dad at the 'sock face', as they called it, and established contact with the few surviving wool spinning mills in Yorkshire. She visited them regularly, made some useful contacts and gained valuable knowledge about the different British wools, becoming experienced at negotiating deals for the bulk purchase of sock yarn.

Back at the factory, they gradually converted most of their machinery to manufacture woollen socks. These were no more profitable than their synthetic sports sock range, but they were much more ecologically sustainable. Tabby and her dad felt that in a small way, they were benefitting British sheep farmers whilst helping to save the planet too.

Tabby's mum slowly came to accept her daughter's

newfound confidence. Though having never learned to drive herself, she was envious of her independence. Initially, she was hostile to the changes Tabby instigated in the business, but with her father's full support, Tabby was able to continue with her goal of making the 'Bleakstones Range' a success.

Whenever Tabatha was in Yorkshire on business, she would either stay at the cottage or, if that was let, in Edna and Bob's guest bedroom. She still loved working with the sheep and the farming life, and every time she visited Rossington, she brought numerous pairs of thick woollen socks as gifts for all her friends, as they were perfect for wearing with wellies.

She continued to keep in touch with Robert by letter. Alun and his unnamed girlfriend had twins, Charlotte and Emily. The couple weren't keen on taking on the farm, so they went to live in a cottage in Rossington, where Alun got a job as a worm drench salesman for an agricultural drug company.

With Bob coming up to retirement, Robert gradually took over the running of the farm, but not on his own. He and Andie were now married, and Andie enjoyed farming, especially the sheep management. She and Tabby got on like a house on fire.

One day, Tabby received a phone call from Robert. "We are throwing a surprise birthday party for Giff in the barn at the weekend," he said. "Do say you will come. Everyone will be there."

"Oh, yes, please," said Tabby without hesitation. "How old will he be?"

"Well, it's special like, he will be forty."

Tabby couldn't hide her surprise. With his unshaven, weather-beaten face and his old-fashioned mannerisms and dialogue, she had assumed he was much older, even though he was so strong and agile. It had come as a shock to learn he was only nine years older than her.

"I... I thought he was a similar age to my dad," Tabby stammered, before instantly regretting saying it.

Robert laughed, said his goodbyes and rang off.

In the run up to the party, Tabby baked a large batch of Fat Ratties to take with her. She left home early on Saturday morning to make the long drive up to Yorkshire. She was looking forward to seeing everyone, and she also took with her a large selection of her woollen 'welly socks' to distribute amongst the guests. She took a long time deciding what to wear, but in the end opted for jeans (much to her mother's disapproval), a floaty red top and a soft woollen wrap woven from black Hebridean wool. Even in the summer, she knew how cold it could get in a barn on the top of the Pennines.

The sun had come out by the time Tabby arrived at Cote Farm in the afternoon. As she parked in the designated field, which was out of sight of the lane so as not to give away the secret when Bob arrived with the birthday boy, Robert came hurrying over to greet her.

"I'm so glad you made it, Tabby," he said. "Giff just thinks he's coming over for a small family do, but we have built a bar in the barn and our Alun is the DJ for the evening. We've got a bouncy castle in the back field for the kids, and me mam has been making food all day. Come and see."

The big barn doors were closed, so Robert opened the small access door in the corner, and they climbed inside. The huge barn had been cleared and swept for the occasion and was decorated with balloons, coloured lights and a banner declaring, "Happy 40th birthday!" Bales of straw had been placed around the edges to provide seating and there was a makeshift dancefloor in the middle of the room. Alun had set up his DJ equipment in one corner and a bar made from pallets occupied another. Trestle tables covered with white tablecloths had been positioned along one wall for all the party food. It all looked splendid.

A number of guests had already arrived, including Jamil, who came rushing over to see Tabby. "Look at you!" he said. "You have changed so much. You seem to have grown taller and you look so well. Come and meet my two sons. My wife is at home with our new baby."

The two boys, aged seven and nine, were delightful, and Tabby decided there and then to design a range of woollen socks just for kids.

Hazel and Jeff were also at the party. Jeff was dressed in black as usual, but Hazel had changed dramatically. She had abandoned her dreadlocks and wore her hair in a short blond urchin cut that suited her elfin features. She had forgone her piercings and was wearing a long yellow kaftan with strappy sandals. They rushed over to greet Tabby. Jeff couldn't wait to tell her that Hazel had graduated from university and had a placement as a student teacher in the English department at the local comprehensive.

"Oh, that's wonderful, congratulations, Hazel," said Tabby, feeling full of admiration. "I love the new look as well; it really suits you."

"Thanks, Tabby. I changed my image a little bit for my new job, and Jeff likes it as well."

Suddenly, the small door of the barn opened, letting in a shaft of light. Alun climbed in waving his arms and calling for silence. "They are here, so shush everyone. I am going to turn out the lights."

The guests stood in the darkness for what seemed like an age while trying to keep the excited children calm. The small door opened, and Bob stepped through followed by Giff.

"What I want to show you is in here," said Bob in a loud theatrical voice. This was the signal for Alun to switch on the lights.

"Happy birthday!" everyone cried in unison, startling Giff, who looked rather like a deer caught in headlights. He stared at the crowd in disbelief. "You buggers," he muttered under his breath.

The music started and there were silly games for the children. Bob declared the makeshift bar open. Tabby sat down in a corner and was enjoying the general frivolity when Giff arrived with a drink in each hand and sat down beside her. He didn't say anything except "Cheers!" as he presented her with the bitter in a plastic pint glass. He took a long swallow of his beer and sighed. They sat in silence, sipping and watching the dancefloor. Tabby noticed that Giff was smartly dressed in a pair of well-fitting moleskin trousers and a crisp cotton check shirt. He'd had a haircut and was clean shaven. His new look had taken years off him.

After a while, the party food for the children arrived and it was devoured in no time. There was to be a barbeque later in the evening for the adults. Whilst the children sang *Happy Birthday*, Edna brought in the splendid cake, which was studded with lighted candles. She called Giff over.

"Won't be long, Tiddles," he said, as he rushed off to get this formality over as quickly as possible. He blew out the candles and everyone cheered and shouted, "Speech, speech!"

"Unaccustomed as I am to public speaking," began Giff, and the crowd jeered. "I would like to thank Edna and Bob for arranging this humiliation for me on my fortieth birthday. Forty, I understand, is the new fifty."

Tabby blushed. Robert must have told him what she had blurted out on the phone.

"Thank you all for coming, and please enjoy yourselves," Giff continued.

Everyone clapped, the music started, and Giff walked over to Tabby. To her surprise, he invited her to dance. They jiggled about self-consciously, grinning and singing along. Alun then changed the tempo and played the old favourite, *Lady in Red*. Tabby turned to return to her bale of straw, but Giff put his arm around her and gently drew her to him for a slow dance. Tabby relaxed and enjoyed the moment. Looking over Giff's shoulder, she saw Robert and Jamil laughing and giving her the thumbs up behind Giff's back, which brought back memories of the dinner party at Bleakstones Farm so long ago.

When the song ended, Giff led Tabby back to their strawbale, and they sat down. "How about coming up to stay for tupping time, lass?"

"Yes, please," whispered Tabby, relieved to note the absence of Giff's usual agricultural ambience. She rested her head on his shoulder and smiled happily as she snuggled up to him.

'Tupping Time', for anyone who has not already guessed, is when the ram is put in with the ewes, usually in November, so that the lambs are born in April the following year.

Acknowledgments

Thank you to Danielle at Wrate's Editing Services for all her help and encouragement.

Thanks also to Nathan Martin, from Purple Demand, for all his vital IT support. And to Barry Wood, for the photograph we used to create the book cover.

My special thanks go to everyone at Bullion Farm, where I was first introduced to the excitement and the addictive nature of sheep farming, and to Gib Farm for the hands-on experience with all the terrors and delights of lambing in the Pennines.

About the Author

B.T. Fisher was born in Bolton, Lancashire, where she began her career in the Civil Service. After transferring to a new posting in West Yorkshire, she found the area so stunning that she decided to stay, and she bought a weavers' cottage in the Pennine Hills, where she still lives today. She began helping out on neighbouring farms, and in order to widen her knowledge, completed a City and Guilds course in Agriculture. Her interest in all types of textile crafts led her to hand spinning and an appreciation of all things woolly. Although she has written several short stories and articles, mostly textile related, *A Week in the Pennines* is her first novel.

Printed in Great Britain
by Amazon